FIC
DEE

NOV 0 7 2012

DATE DUE

JAN 0 3			
JAN 1 0 2013			
FEB 2 3 2013			
SEP 0 7 2016			

PRINTED IN U.S.A.

**BLUE ISLAND
PUBLIC LIBRARY**

The most abundant unconditional love, is the love of Jesus Christ. It is my prayer that you know HIM. I pray for you and I praise God for you. If by chance you do not know Him as your personal Lord and Savior please read Romans 10:9 TEV "If you confess that Jesus is Lord AND Believe that God raised HIM from death, you will be SAVED." If you read, recited and believed this verse, then you are saved! Please find a bible-based fellowship. Praise God! God bless you!

In loving memory of
Georgia Evelyn Harling Roland
May 15, 1920 – July 11, 2012

Bountifully Blessed Woman Enterprises

PO Box 394

Asheville, NC 28802

Written by Allyson M. Deese

Published by Bountifully Blessed Woman Enterprises

Edited by Isaiah David Paul

Originally published as Love.com by Lady Leo Publishing (2010) Edited by EBM Professional Services for Lady Leo Publishing

Original rights reverted back to author January 2011

First edition by Bountifully Blessed Woman Enterprises 2012

HISLOVE.COM is a work of fiction. Names, characters, places and incidents are either products of the author's imagination or are used fictitiously. Any resemblance to actual persons, living or dead, business establishments, events or locales is entirely coincidental.

Copyright © 2012 by Allyson M. Deese

All rights reserved, including the right of reproduction, in whole or in part, in any form. No parts of this book may be reproduced in any form or by any means without the prior written consent of the publisher.

Chapter One

Laisha

I bet you have a beautiful smile.

Covering her mouth with her right hand, Laisha Bowman giggled like a schoolgirl before typing her reply.

Says who?

She was way too shy to talk face-to-face with anyone about anything except business and a good book.

She had been chatting with **Techy4Christ** for four weeks and every time they talked online, no matter what they were talking about, he made her heart skip a beat. *What is it about this man whose real name I don't even know, that makes me feel this way? I wish I knew,* she wondered. Laisha Bowman was a thirty year old single gal who shared a moderately-sized condo with a goldfish; no kids, no man, no roommate, just her and the goldfish. She spent her days climbing the corporate ladder at a Fortune 500 advertising company. Most of her evenings were spent in front of the computer within the confinement of her home or with her nose in an engaging novel. Other than church, and her weekly Sistahz Only Book Club meetings, indulging in her online persona: **Bountifully Blessed Sista** was the highlight of her life. She wished she was vibrant as her online persona.

On paper, her life looked like it was all pulled together. Laisha was up for a promotion at work and on the career path of her dreams. Imagine, a Southern gal from Asheville, North Carolina, an executive-in-the-making at a major advertising company in beautiful Atlanta.

She already owned a home, a fairly new car, and even some rental property. She'd never been married and had no kids, so, her life was free of the baby-daddy drama. Standing at five foot five, Laisha had an adorable face with sweet, smiling eyes and was very curvaceous. Sadly she was unable to see and appreciate her appearance. *What man wanted a woman who weighed as much as she did?*

She used to enjoy the single life. It's just moments like this when she missed the feeling of a man most. And right now, **Techy4Christ** was looking kinda good to a girl who hadn't been on a date in a year. Laisha has never been attracted to a white man before and it felt kind of weird, but she liked him. Well, at least what she knew of him so far.

Techy4Christ : What are you reading this week cutie?

Bountifully Blessed Sista: I'm reading *Street Disciples* by Isaiah David Paul.

Techy4Christ: ☺ I heard that his work was good.

Bountifully Blessed Sista: Now, you've got me curious. What are you reading?

Techy4Christ: Well beautiful, I'm currently reading *Lying To Myself* by Linda R. Herman.

Techy4Christ: Are you up for a lil e-chess?

He's always down for this. If only this wasn't some cyber thing. If only this was the real deal. *But, what if this was the real deal?* Would she make time for him if he were literally sitting beside her? Her head said no, and her heart didn't seem so pleased with that answer, but she was being honest. Or was she?

Bountifully Blessed Sista: Maybe a little, I've got to get up early for a meeting.

Techy4Christ: Here's the knight. Your move.

Just as she was getting into the game, he stopped.

Techy4Christ: You won!

Bountifully Blessed Sista: But I didn't even play yet.

Techy4Christ: Because, I don't want to keep you from your sleep. You do have a meeting in the morning. Good night my sweet.

With that, he was gone. Disappointed, she got up from the computer and went down the hall to her bedroom. She tossed and turned for most of the night, for two reasons: one, she knew she really didn't want to end their nightly game, and two, she knew she was lying to him about having a presentation in the morning.

I can't even hold on to a man in cyber land.

**

Laisha arrived at the office around seven-thirty the next morning. Of course the first person she laid eyes on was Devin Kingston. She has such disdain for him that her eyes automatically rolled at the site of him. *God forgive me for my thoughts but I can't stand him!*

"Good morning, Laisha," he said. She could tell he was forcing his fake, cheesy smile. She was sure that he didn't care for her any more than she cared for him.

"Good morning," Laisha mumbled without breaking her stride. She wanted to put as much distance between him and her as she could.

Devin's cubicle was located right across from hers and they were the only two people in the office. As much as she hated to start work so early, she figured it was better than holding a meaningless conversation with him. Apparently, he felt the same way because he didn't breathe another word until their co-workers began filing in the office one by one. He greeted them all with a good morning as they headed to their own cubicles.

She honestly didn't know what started the war between her and Devin. They were both very competitive and equally eager to climb the corporate ladder. As a matter of fact, Devin was her biggest competition. He'd never done anything to personally sabotage her or her career but she just didn't trust him any farther than she could throw him.

Devin was constantly kissing up to and rubbing elbows with upper management. Being that he was a man and Caucasian, she often felt that he had the advantage whereas she, the single, black female was definitely at a major disadvantage having to prove herself as not only a woman, but a black woman. Though she was propositioned on numerous occasions, Laisha decided long ago to let her work speak for her. She wasn't one of those women willing to sleep her way to the top of the ladder only to be snatched back down because of scandal. She fought tooth and nail for every commendation and wasn't going to stop fighting until she reached the top on merit and hard work.

After working non-stop all morning, she realized she was caught up and decided to take a break before lunch, she closed out the program she was in and went to her personal instant messenger to see if she had any messages from her online friend.

A wide, toothy grin covered her face when she saw that he'd wished her a good morning. Hoping he was still on line, she hurriedly typed a reply.

**

Devin

There's my lady love. He smiled to himself.

Devin had been waiting all morning for her to reply to his morning greeting. He couldn't deny it he loved Black women, their curves, beautiful skin, independence, and even the attitude that so many people claimed was a major turn off. For him, it was a turn on because he wanted to know the reason behind the attitude. For him, it was a personal challenge to tame a sassy woman and keep her happy.

Bountifully Blessed Sista: Hey…I'm fine, how are you this morning?

Techy4Christ: I'm okay gorgeous, no scratch that I'm wonderful, now that I'm talking to you.

Bountifully Blessed Sista: You know, you always seem to brighten my day too. ☺

Techy4Christ: Really? Tell me how.

Bountifully Blessed Sista: Of course you do, I wouldn't tell you so if you didn't. My day can be going completely wrong and all I have to do is think of your encouraging words and everything is suddenly all better.

While typing back and forth, Devin glanced over at Laisha and saw that she was smiling from ear to ear about something. *That's a Kodak moment.* Devin assumed it was probably work- related because she didn't strike him as the type to have a social life. Laisha was always the first one in the office, if he didn't arrive seconds before her, and she was the last one to leave. Laisha Bowman was married to her job and he doubted there was a man good enough for a woman so prissy and career-driven. She was probably too much for any man.

Look at her sitting there with her hair pulled back in a tight bun like an old maid. She couldn't have been more than thirty years old, if that, but she carried herself like an old grandmother. Her long hair was always in a bun and her glasses rested on the bridge of her nose. He couldn't remember a time she wore any vibrant colors; with her it was always grays, blacks, and browns. She could definitely stand a makeover, especially her personality. *She could be pretty if she'd loosen up.* When she caught him staring at her, she rolled her eyes and mumbled something under her breath. Devin never understood why she hated him so much but he had to admit that she wasn't his favorite person either. Every time he turned around she was getting a pat on the back for a job well done. As much as he thought did to make good with upper management and she was the one who was always praised.

Devin turned his attention back to his computer screen and noticed the message from **<u>Bountifully Blessed Sista</u>**. She told him she was heading out to lunch and looked forward to their evening chat. He responded that he'd be on pins and needles until then.

He logged off of his computer, picked up his briefcase and headed out to lunch.

"Hold the elevator, please!" Devin yelled as he rushed toward the closing doors. He barely reached it just in time and slid inside thanks to the help of the occupant already on board.

"Thanks," Devin smiled with his head down.

"Umm hmm." He looked up and realized he was alone on the elevator with Laisha.

"Going out for a bite to eat, huh?" He asked, trying to make small talk.

"It is lunchtime."

He decided to ignore her sarcasm and continue the idle chit-chat. "So, what are you having for lunch?"

"Food. Are you having anything other than that?" She cut her eyes at him not hiding the fact that she didn't want to converse with him at all.

He threw his hands up in surrender. "I'm sorry, didn't mean to upset you."

She turned abruptly and glared at him like a parent ready to discipline a disobedient child. "Who said I was upset?"

Devin opened his mouth to respond but she continued on with more questions.

"Did you consider the fact that I just don't want to talk to you? Is it too hard for you to believe that I don't find you a likeable person, Devin?"

He almost asked her who put thumbtacks in her cereal but he knew that would only make matters worse. His father taught him long ago that there's no winning a fight with a woman so the best thing to do is just apologize, even if you don't know what you're apologizing for. Devin made a mental note to thank his father for the advice.

"Laisha, I don't know if we got off on the wrong foot or if I've done anything to offend you. If that's the case, I pray that you forgive me and I hope you enjoy your lunch."

The elevator doors finally opened and without another word, they went their separate ways.

Chapter Two
Laisha

Lord knows I shouldn't have been so mean to him, but I really didn't like the fact that he assumed that I was upset. Devin assuming she was upset; upset her more. The world needed to stop seeing Black women as these angry creatures that are mad at the world because that's the kind of stuff that makes Black women angry.

She decided to freshen up and finalize her lunch plans. She wasn't quite sure what she wanted for lunch but the rumbling in her stomach told her she'd better make up her mind quick, fast, and in an urgent hurry. It would have been nice to go to mid-day bible study, but she knew that she couldn't take a two hour lunch today.

For Laisha, staring in the mirror was like staring face to face with her paternal grandmother. Even though her hair was shoulder length, she rarely wore it down, especially at the office. She just didn't find that to be professional so she always secured it in a bun. Rather than contacts, she wore reading glasses in the office, and as much as she loved bright colors, such as yellows, oranges, and pinks, she stuck to the basic business colors. She felt that if she wanted to be taken seriously, she had to look the part. It didn't get more serious than a thirty year-old woman hiding her vibrate self in corporate America.

After brushing her bun and reapplying her lip gloss, her mind was made up about lunch. She walked briskly around the corner to her favorite diner where they made the best sub sandwiches, the sweetest lemonade, and cake so moist and sweet you'd slap your mother for trying to get the last bite.

"Hello, welcome to Cindy's!" the young waitress greeted her. She wasn't one of the usual servers. "How many in your party?"

Is she blind? She looked around because she didn't remember anyone walking in with her and even though she was thick, there was no way anyone would mistake her for two people. Rather than answer her verbally, Laisha held up one finger and prayed the girl could count that high. She wasn't a mean person but the encounter with Devin had left a bitter taste in her mouth and she was a prayer away from hurting someone's feelings.

"Follow me." The hostess led Laisha to the bar where the TV was located. She climbed on the barstool and nearly fell off when she realized she was sitting next to Devin.

She felt that it was bad enough that her cubicle sat across from his cubicle at the office. Now she had to sit next to him during her lunch break as well. *Unbelievable!* She scanned the crowded diner for an empty table since the bar was full. *Just my luck, nothing is available.*

"May I take your order please?" Ms. Sunshine sang as she smiled ear to ear while popping her gum. "Yes, I'd like a lemonade as well as a glass of water, a ham and cheese sub with special seasoning rather than mayo, and a slice of red velvet cake, please." Devin looked up at the sound of Laisha's voice but when his eyes met hers, he quickly turned away and diverted his attention on the meal before him. *Thank you.*

She focused her attention on the TV while waiting for her food. It was awkward sitting next to Devin while trying to feign interest in the news. She cared about world events but in five minutes time, she'd seen the same story twice.

"You eat here a lot?" *Here we go. Why is he so determined to make conversation with me?*

"Actually, I do. Why?"

"I'm just asking a question Laisha. It's my first time here and the food is delicious."

The server arrived with her food and she turned her attention to her meal. She said grace and then took a bite of her sub and she forgot all about what's his face sitting next to her. Not even he could ruin the goodness of her lunch.

A few bites later she heard Devin clear his throat. When she looked over he was pulling money from his wallet to place on the table before climbing off the barstool.

"Enjoy your lunch."

She was certain that she could enjoy it a lot better with him gone. She then took an even bigger bite of the sub and chased it down with some sweet lemonade. It was like a slice of heaven.

Chapter Three

Devin

Laisha was in a class all by herself and surely a man would have his work cut out for him if he dared to date her.

Devin often found himself staring longingly at her. But no sooner than she'd turn around and give him the evil eye, his sweet daydream would turn into a live nightmare. It was amazing how one woman could be so beautiful on the outside and so ugly on the inside at the same time.

Back in his cubicle, Devin decided to put the finishing touches on an ad presentation he'd been working on. Devin was sure it would earn him the promotion he was in the running for against none other than Laisha. She was his biggest competition and he had to admit, she was very good at what she did. Not to say he wasn't but he knew that he had to work extra hard to get the promotion.

As Devin worked on his project, he thought about his daughter and wondered how her day at school was going. Abby was his one and only child and the best thing to come of his ten year marriage to

Morgan, his ex-wife. That marriage had turned out to be a big disaster.

Morgan and Devin had been forced to be childhood sweethearts. Their families had been close since their mothers met in the delivery room and as far as he could remember his family memories, he also had memories of Morgan and her family. They even shared bath times together as toddlers and every first event for one was shared by both.

The families made it no secret that they wanted Morgan and him to date. Not that he minded so much because Morgan was a beautiful girl. She was petite with blonde hair, blue eyes, and fair skin. She had all the beauty and grace of a supermodel and Morgan was also very intelligent. She was the perfect choice as far as his family was concerned.

Morgan and he dated all through high school and married after college and Abby was born two years later. The first five years of their marriage was good, nothing to marvel about but they were doing quite well, living the American dream so to speak. They shared an immaculate home and two healthy incomes, not to mention a beautiful daughter. Sadly they were missing God's guidance and neither of them knew how to bring that to the table.

He began focus on God and his career in advertising and Morgan was making a name for herself in the entertainment industry appearing regularly on a local soap opera. It wasn't long before she was swept off her feet by a tall man with olive skin, jet-black hair, and green eyes. After a five-year affair that Devin was very much aware of, Morgan took their daughter and left to be with the true love of her life.

Devin tried his best to hate Morgan but in all honesty, all he could do was pray for her. He actually admired her for getting out of the pre-arranged marriage to pursue her definition of true happiness. The only thing he really hated was not being able to spend every day with his daughter. Devin's love for Abby was genuine; she was his entire world.

Devin was just grateful that he was able to be there for Abby and teach her of the love of Jesus Christ.

Adjusting to bachelorhood had been hard for him, and a year later, he still struggled with being single.

The dating scene was a little crazy in his opinion so he often chatted online with prospects that he rarely met. After two uneventful meetings, he was a bit apprehensive about meeting anyone else from the cyber world. Even though he had to admit, his latest cyber-friend had him curious to know what she looked like in person. He'd never dated a Black woman before but had to admit he'd always been attracted to them.

Closing his eyes, he leaned back in his chair and thought back to some of his online chats with **<u>Bountifully Blessed Sista</u>**. A smile graced his face as his thoughts became more and more filled with sweet daydreams of her.

"Maybe you should get in a bed!" His eyes flew open at the sound of Laisha's voice. She'd caught him dosing off right there in the office. He prayed she wouldn't go running and screaming to the big dogs and have him fired.

"Laisha, I-let me apologize. I must have dosed off or something."

Devin needed to make it the best ever if he had a chance of getting the promotion or at the very least, keeping his job.

Laisha

Just as she was getting Devin off of her mind, her cyber-love popped online.

Techy4Christ: Hey gorgeous. I was just thinking about you.

Bountifully Blessed Sista: Hey, what were you thinking about me?

She was always curious to know what he was thinking because she always felt so beautiful when he shared his thoughts.

Techy4Christ: I was thinking about how beautiful you must look when you are in a serene place or in a state of worship.

Bountifully Blessed Sista: Wow, you were thinking all of that?

Mmm... Now I'm blushing at work.

Bountifully Blessed Sista: You really know how to make a girl forget all about her bad day.

Techy4Christ: When can we meet or at least talk on the phone.

Bountifully Blessed Sista: Soon sweeetie, soon. Well I've got to get back to work. My boss just faxed me a new assignment. *hugs* Talk to you later? ☺

Then she realized it wasn't her fax machine that was going off, it was Devin's. She'd probably be stuck with the worst assignment from the bottom of the pile. While all the "good ol' boys" got the cream of the crop assignments. *I'm gonna own an even better company one day. A kingdom business.*

After an uneventful afternoon that ended with her rolling her eyes at Devin the snake, she was happy to hit the elevator and make her way to the parking garage.

It was Thursday so she had to rush home to change for her Sistaz Only book club meeting with featured guest author, Linda R. Herman. She was so excited about meeting the lady who penned stories that inspired her to want to make a difference.

She changed out of her boring business suit and slipped into a pair of jeans and a light blue blouse. She removed the bobby pens from her tight bun and brushed her long hair down into a wrap that hugged her round face. Smiling at her reflection, she realized she looked like a totally different person. Without a second to spare, she grabbed her copy of *Consequences* off the nightstand and rushed outside to her shiny Acura.

Their book club meetings were being held at a local poetry bar. The meeting was scheduled for an hour and was set to conclude thirty minutes before the poetry bar officially opened. Some nights the women would sit in the back of the bar and listen to the spoken-word artists. Laisha's favorite was Casche Russell, a Nubian goddess who shared her painful childhood through spoken word. Her words were so powerful that there was rarely a dry eye in the crowd after she spoke.

She was the last to arrive at the meeting, right on time.

"And last but not least," Tinisha giggled as she introduced her, "this is Laisha Bowman, another avid reader and lover of African American fiction. Laisha is in the advertising field so it's really admirable that she commits to reading a book a week with such a full schedule."

"Hello, Laisha. I'm Linda R. Herman," the beautiful author greeted as she shook her hand. Linda was a confident plus size sister with a sharp haircut.

"It's truly an honor to meet you, Ms. Herman. I loved *Consequences*."

"Please, call me Linda, Laisha. And guess what? The sequel is now available!" Squeals of delight could be heard bouncing off the walls after Linda's announcement. Every book club member bought an autographed copy of the novel before the meeting officially began.

"It certainly inspired me to talk to my husband and for us to go get tested together. Jocelyn shared, as she was a salon owner on husband number three.

"So, it was a win-win situation," Linda laughed. "You both got tested and it brought you both closer to each other, right?"

"Sure you right!" Jocelyn slapped Linda a hi-five while they all smiled and nodded in agreement. Each woman sat on the edge of her seat, as Linda spoke on the importance of taking care of themselves as well as communicating with their partners. It was the most informative meeting they had ever had.

"Are you going to stay for spoken word, Laisha?" Tinisha inquired as everyone else packed up to leave. She was the only one of the group members that Laisha occasionally spoke to outside the book meetings. A beautiful woman in her early thirties,

Tinisha was married and worked from home. Even though she couldn't say that they were friends, she was the closest thing Laisha had to a friend. Had Laisha allowed herself to have friends, Tinisha would have been her best friend.

"I think I will."

"Mind if I join you? Linda's going up tonight to recite her poem that she dedicated to her late grandmother and I don't want to miss it."

"Sure thing, Tinisha. I can't wait to hear her poem and I'm looking forward to reading the book." Even though it seemed a bit much to read a book in a week's time, the ladies always did it no matter what they had going on at work or in their personal lives. They met every week to talk about the books. Sometimes they were fortunate enough to have the author sit down with them, like this week with Ms. Herman who agreed to return the following Thursday to discuss latest book.

After an enchanting evening, she returned home and logged on to her computer. Laisha smiled from ear to ear when she noticed she had a message from **Techy4Christ**.

As usual he asked, How was the rest of your day?

Boldly, she responded, Almost as good as it would be if you were a permanent fixture in my life. Then she prayed he was still online and would respond. She thought she was ready to meet him and let go of some of her fears.

**

Chapter Four

Devin

There's my baby.

Techy4Christ: Hey Beautiful! Are you honestly ready for me?

Bountifully Blessed Sista: Yes baby, I want to see you. That's if you want to see me.

Techy4Christ: Of course I want to. What man in his right mind wouldn't want to see natural beauty like yours, Babydoll. I want to show you how beautiful I think you are.

Bountifully Blessed Sista: Just that beautiful thought, made me ☺.

***

Laisha

Laisha really wanted cyber-guy to be hers. She was determined that there wasn't going to be anything to stop her from loving this man if he really wanted her.

Bountifully Blessed Sista: I'll let you see in the morning. We can exchange pictures then.

Techy4Christ: Fair enough. I can't wait to see you, beautiful you. Babydoll, I hate to cut this short, but I've got to get dressed. My daughter will be over here in a few minutes. I can't wait until the morning.

Bountifully Blessed Sista: I can't wait either. Good night.

Devin

Almost as soon as Devin signed off there was a knock at the door. He threw on his oversized t-shirt, and opened the door and his heart immediately melted. There stood his little princess, Abby, at her mother's side.

"Hi Daddy!" Abby squealed as she catapulted through the door, tackling her father, almost knocking him backward.

"Hi there, Princess." She gave him one of those bear hugs that helped make living worthwhile for Devin. In return, he squeezed her as tightly as he could without breaking her bones.

"I missed you Daddy," she declared before running past Devin and into the living room.

Thankfully he had logged out of his account on his laptop, because that was the first thing that Abby dashed to. "We really appreciate you taking her a day early. Everything was so last minute. Esteban is full of surprises."

Devin rolled his eyes and waved his hand dismissively. "She's my daughter, Morgan. You don't have to thank me; it's my pleasure to have an extra day to spend with Princess Abby."

"I know, Devin. I was just saying…"

He interrupted by changing the subject. "You look beautiful as always, Morgan. Won't you come in?"

Morgan thanked him with a gracious smile and nod of her head before stepping inside his modest, but nice apartment. She really did look beautiful. Morgan looked like she was still on cloud nine and truth be told he was happy for her. If she couldn't be happy with him, at least she was happy with Esteban.

"So, how is life treating you?" Devin asked, digging his idle hands into his pockets.

"I'm well thank you, and yourself?"

"I'm good, can't complain." Their general conversation was always awkward, other than Abby they still didn't have much more to talk about, very much the way their conversations went when they were married.

"Daddy! Guess what?" Abby squealed. She was bubbling over with some information that she couldn't wait to share.

"No, Abby, I'll tell Daddy later." Morgan gave Abby a very stern look that peaked Devin's curiosity. *What kind of secret are they keeping?* Devin wondered.

"But, Mommy, I want to tell Daddy that I'm going to have a baby brother or sister," Abby whined.

Oh man...a baby. Morgan and I once talked of having a second baby together. That news had Devin in a bit of a shock. Even though he was over Morgan he never considered the possibility of her and the *new* Mr. having more kids.

After a few minutes of awkward silence he dug his right hand out of his pocket and extended it to Morgan. "Well, I must say congratulations are in order, Morgan. How special for you and Esteban. I hope he treasures this time as I did when you were carrying Abby."

"Thanks Don." She shook his hand and smiled. "Can I use your restroom before I split?"

"Sure Morgan, you know where it is."

Once her mother was out of the room, Abby asked, "Daddy, aren't you excited? I'm going to be a big sister."

"Yeah, Abby, I'm thrilled." Quickly changing the subject, he asked, "Have you had dinner Miss Abby?"

"Yes Daddy. I had some of Mommy's vegan pizza." *Yuck, to me, vegan and pizza don't belong in the same sentence.*

"Abby, you like that type of food?" Devin just couldn't imagine his little girl liking that stuff. He sure never cared for it when he and Morgan were married.

"Daddy I love it, the tofu cheese taste just like regular cheese." Abby grinned up at him revealing her missing front tooth. *My baby girl is sure to be a heartbreaker.*

"Do you want some dessert? Grandma sent over a cheesecake just for you." Abby's face lit up like the harvest moon.

"With strawberries and whip cream?"

"Sure pumpkin. Why not?"

After Morgan hugged Abby good-bye, she thanked Devin again for taking her a day early and left.

As Devin enjoyed cheesecake with his daughter, he couldn't help but wonder what his online goddess was doing.

Chapter Five

Laisha

Laisha hoped her cyber-boo was enjoying his time with his daughter, but she was already missing his words that always warmed her heart. So she decided to lie in bed and read a couple chapters of Linda's new book, until she felt herself get sleepy. She laid her head back on the fluffiest pillow in her bed and commenced to reading. Once she enjoyed a couple of chapters, she turned over and went to sleep.

***

Laisha couldn't wait to get to work the next morning. She rushed through her usual coffee, and actually skipped her normal routine of stopping by the little bakery on the corner owned by Michelle. Michelle Barrett was very friendly and always had kind words for her. She had once thought about inviting Michelle to poetry nights but, of course, she was always too shy to say anything but how good the bear claws were each morning before disappearing out the doors and down the street to her office building.

Arriving at the office, Devin's was the first face she saw. "Good morning, Laisha," he smiled.

Not even he could ruin her mood that day. "Good morning, Devin. How are you?" she asked while sliding into her cubicle. She heard him answer but wasn't truly interested in his reply. She tuned him out and logged on to her computer. She was eager to exchange photos with the man she deemed her special friend. They were going to finally lay eyes on each other.

Devin

Wow, he thought, *Laisha sure seemed to be in a good mood. Heck, maybe she met someone.* Shaking his head he laughed and returned to his true thoughts which were all about the chocolate diva whose picture he couldn't wait to see.

Devin turned to log into his account. No sooner than he did, there was an instant messenger alarm, alerting him to new mail.

Bountifully Blessed Sista: Good morning love.

Devin smiled.

Techy4Christ: Good morning sweetheart. How are you today?

Bountifully Blessed Sista: I'm okay. How are you?

Techy4Christ: I'll be even better when I see you beautiful.

Bountifully Blessed Sista: Oh really?

Techy4Christ: Really, let's send our pictures at the same time.

Bountifully Blessed Sista: <sending picture>

Techy4Christ: <sending picture>

Devin rubbed his hands together as he waited for the file to completely download. He looked over at Laisha and noticed that she too was smiling, sitting on the edge of her seat waiting for something to pop up on her computer screen.

I wonder what she's working on that has her so giddy. Devin watched as her beautiful smile transformed into an ungodly scowl, meaner than the ones he was accustomed to seeing on her face. She turned to look at him and if looks could kill, Devin's family would have had to make funeral arrangements.

He opened his mouth to ask what he'd done but heard a buzz from his computer indicating his file had completely downloaded. Devin turned to the screen and his eyes nearly popped out of his head. *Oh my God…it's Laisha and she's gorgeous outside of work. I always knew she was beautiful, but wow! Who would of thought that she would be the one I had been dreaming of?*

I have to tell her how I feel about her. Devin slowly turned his head to face Laisha. *Oh man, she looks repulsed.* He rose from his chair and walked toward her cubicle.

"Laisha, can I speak to you for a moment please?" He whispered, praying she would be open minded enough to listen.

"What?" She snapped. *Here we go; she has an attitude already.* "What do you want Devin?"

Refusing to beat around the bush, Devin's reply was simple. "You." He felt like that said it all. "I want you, Laisha. I admit I was surprised to find out you were my dream woman but, yes, I want you. Now more than ever. I've always been attracted to you and, now that I know that you love Christ just as much as I do, and…"

"Well, Devin, I don't feel the same way about you." She hissed through clenched teeth. "You're the last person I want to think about falling in love with!" She jumped up from her chair, grabbed her purse and briefcase and stormed away nearly knocking Devin over in the process. Devin watched helplessly as she exited by way of elevator without looking at him. In one breath, she'd crushed his dreams.

Laisha

Of all people, why did it have to be Devin? There is no way I could even think about having a relationship with that arrogant man! I'll remain celibate and lonely forever, before, I consider him to be a potential life mate.

She was sitting at her desk in her home office fuming. She'd called back to the office to let her supervisor know she'd taken a sick day and would be working from home until further notice. Being that Laisha rarely missed a day's work, the boss didn't hassle her. Instead he told her to take care of herself and feel better. Laisha thanked him and hung up the phone.

Unable to focus and get any work done, she sat drumming her fingernails on the desk top until an instant message from Devin popped up on her screen. She moved the cursor to erase the message but decided against it. She clicked open and read his message.

Techy4Christ: Laisha, I know you may not want me, but I really do want you. I want to get to know you. All of you. Please talk to me. Devin

She most definitely wasn't talking to him. To be honest, she really didn't know how to feel, but she definitely wasn't ready to talk to him. Just as she was getting ready to shut down her computer for the day, she received another instant message from Devin.

Techy4Christ: Laisha please call me at 456-555-7842.

Laisha fished her Smartphone out of her purse and added the number to her contacts. She had no intentions of using the number, but still she saved it in her phone.

I can't believe that I saved his number, it's not like I'm ever calling him, she thought as she cleaned her townhome from top to bottom. She considered calling Tinisha; because she sure could use a friend and Tinisha was the first person that came to mind. She picked up her cell phone and started dialing her number but quickly dismissed that idea. It was Friday and Tinisha likely had plans with her family.

Laisha didn't feel as close to the other members of the book club. Sure they were nice enough but she didn't know them well enough to blab her business to, because there were some heavy gossipers in the group. The last thing she needed or wanted was every sister in the book club knowing all about her personal life, or lack thereof.

With no other options, Laisha called her mother.

"Hello?" The phone was answered on the second ring.

"Momma, hey, it's me."

"Me who?" Laisha knew her mother was purposely trying to get on her nerves by playing games and it drove her crazy.

"It's your daughter Ma. I called because I'm coming home to spend the weekend with you." *I definitely need to get a life.*

"Is something wrong baby?" Lenora Elaine Bowman asked. Sadly, they didn't spend a lot of time together so the news of Laisha's pending visit was a bit of a surprise to her mother.

"Nothing's wrong, Ma," Laisha lied. "I just haven't seen you in awhile and I don't have any plans for the weekend."

Her mother laughed hysterically as if she were on stage at the Apollo telling the funniest jokes ever. "Girl, do you ever have plans? Last time I saw you Lai, you were bigger than a house and I bet you still dating Ben and Jerry."

"Ben and Jerry?" Laisha walked blindly into that wise crack.

"Oh my gosh!" The older woman wailed. "The ice cream, Lai! Girl, you 'bout sharp as a rubber ball. Let me get off this phone so I can fix your room up. Have a safe trip."

Lenora hung up laughing and didn't even say good-bye. It never once crossed her mind how her jokes hurt her to the core. She understood how people died of broken hearts because she'd been dying of one since she was a preteen. She prayed that her mother would one day change, but, she had long since stop holding her breath waiting for it to happen.

The majority of her weight gain started when she hit puberty. Every time she had a problem she fed her pain and cried herself to sleep. Most of her tears were caused by the hormonal changes girls go through. The kids her age and older weren't too fond of her. They made fun of her dark skin and the out-of-style clothes that she wore. Of course the picking got worse when she gained all the weight because then she didn't just feel like she was black and ugly; she felt like she was *fat*, black, and ugly.

Her mother didn't make matters any better. The pain and bitterness her mother felt towards Laisha's father was taken out on her only child because in her mother's words, she looked just like the black, no-good bastard. When he left them, she left her, who often wondered if her momma loved her at all or if she enjoyed hurting her every chance she got in a feeble attempt to get back at a man who abandoned them both. She hadn't seen or heard from her father in over twenty years; didn't even know if the man was alive or dead. *Wherever he is, he's no doubt happier and more content than I am.*

She packed enough clothing and toiletries for the weekend and threw her luggage in the trunk of her car. She closed her eyes and prayed to God for mercy, kindness, and restraint not to go off on her mother before backing out of her driveway.

Chapter Six

When Laisha drove up to her childhood home in Asheville, she sat in her car for a few minutes staring up at her bedroom window. She actually visualized her younger self standing in the window staring down at her current self. She saw the pain in her own eyes. Home was the last place she wanted to be but she couldn't handle being alone at the time. Being in her mother's company, she prayed, was the lesser of the two evils.

Slowly, she got out the car, popped the trunk, and grabbed her suitcase. *Lord, I need you.* Her journey up the walkway was deliberately long. The closer she got to the house, the more she thought about turning around and driving back to Atlanta.

Before she reached the top step the front door flew open and there stood her beautiful mother with a cigarette dangling from her lips. At age fifty-three, she still looked good. She was tall and slender with skin the color of honey that glowed. Her once long hair was now cut in a short bob that fit her face perfectly. Everything about her mother was perfect;

well until her mouth opened and the ugliness from inside overshadowed her outer beauty.

"Lai, baby, you look-"

"What, fat?" Laisha interrupted.

Her mother waved her hand dismissively. "Girl, you been fat. I was going to say you look like something is bothering you." She gave Laisha a hug and a pat on her back before stepping aside and allowing her to cross the threshold into the immaculately kept home. As always the house smelled clean like she'd been scrubbing with Pine-Sol all day, and there wasn't a speck of dust in sight.

"Why don't you put your suitcase upstairs in your room and come have some tea with me. Tell me what's troubling you and don't tell me nothing because I know you don't drive all the way to Asheville just to visit me. Shoot, I barely hear from you."

She quietly followed her mother's orders and trekked up the stairs to her room. When she opened the door she was embraced by a strong dose of nostalgia. Her room was just as she had left it years earlier. It looked as if she'd left for school and came back home to the purple and lavender room with her favorite teddy bears lined up on her bed.

 She dropped her suitcase and made slow steps toward her queen-sized bed. Laisha ran her hand across the reversible comforter and smiled. The lavender side was facing up and her purple pillow shams rested on top of the comforter. Lavender curtains covered the two windows and the room smelled of fresh lilacs. Looking over at the desk, she saw a fresh bouquet of flowers in her favorite vase.

 The walls were covered with posters of Michael Jackson, New Edition, and Boyz II Men, all the men that she fantasized were singing for her ears only years ago.

 After unpacking, she washed up and joined her mother in the kitchen for tea as she'd instructed.

 "Thanks for the flowers Momma, they're beautiful."

 "I remember you always liked having fresh flowers in your room." Lenora took a long sip of tea. She wasn't used to her mother being cordial so she was actually at a loss for words.

After several minutes of silence Lenora cleared her throat and asked, "So, what's troubling you, Lai? You know I don't like when you're so quiet. This house is always quiet now that it's just me here." She dropped her head and for a minute Laisha thought her mother might actually cry. "It's too quiet."

"Momma, is something wrong?" Laisha reached across the table and covered her mother's hand with hers but her mother quickly snatched away.

"What you mean is something wrong? That's what I've been asking you and you still haven't told me!" she snapped.

That's when Laisha knew something was on her mind but dared not ask again. Her mother was back to her old self with her guard up and she wasn't about to have her heart broken, trying to trample it down.

"I met a man on-line, Momma. It felt like we had something good going until-"

"Until what? Until you came to your senses and realized you can't find love on line? What were you thinking? You know you can't just go to hook-up.com and find Mr. Right."

I knew you wouldn't understand. You never do, she thought before defending herself, "I work long hours at the office and I don't have time for dating. There's nothing wrong with meeting a nice man online, besides I met him on a Christian site."

"Girl, who you think you fooling? You hiding behind that computer because of your weight. If you'd lose some weight you'd feel more comfortable meeting a man the old-fashioned way," Lenora stated matter-of-factly.

She had to take slow breaths and remember that the woman sitting across the table from her was her mother. She had to respect her mother even if it was hard to like her at that moment.

"Well, go on. Tell me the rest of the story," her mother insisted while Laisha gathered herself.

She went on to tell her mother how she realized her God-sent, Mr. Right was the man she wanted the least, her co-worker, Devin Kingston.

Lenora calmly set her favorite mug down on the table while Laisha shook like a leaf on a tree. She had no idea what her mother would say next but she knew it wouldn't be nice, not after hearing that Devin was white and she thought she had real feelings for him.

"You mean to tell me you're sitting here all sad over some white man who you can't stand in person but think you developed feelings for over your computer? A white man? Didn't you know he was white before you found out he was your co-worker?"

"Yes, Momma, I knew he was white but I had no idea it…" as usual she cut Laisha off.

"It doesn't matter!" she yelled! "It doesn't matter if he's Devin or Ronald McDonald, Lai! He's white! Your father left us for a white woman and now here you go wanting you a white man. As black as your skin is, you mean to tell me that black folks ain't good enough for you?"

She opened her mouth to speak but her mother continued her ranting. "I do declare you remind me more and more of your no-good daddy every time I look at you!"

"Is that why you hate me so much?! I've prayed and prayed that you would stop hating me, but I see that I was just wasting my breath. " Laisha screamed as tears danced down her cheeks.

"Hate you?" Lenora's eyes searched her daughter's as she waited for her to respond.

"Yes, hate me. You've been on my case since Daddy left, Momma. You act as if you're the only one hurt by his leaving." She stood up and pounded her fist into the table, spilling tea as both mugs tumbled over. "He didn't just leave you; he left me, too! You never asked how I was feeling. All you did was ridicule me and remind me every day that I was just like my no good daddy!"

"Laisha, I-"

"No, shut up , Momma!" After years of sitting by quietly while her mother robbed her of her self-esteem, she'd had quite enough. She didn't mean to disrespect her mother, but, she was at her wits end and her mother was not helping matters. "I came to you because I didn't have anyone else to turn to. Thanks to you, I don't know how to make friends because I'm always so insecure thinking everybody is going to make fun of my dark skin and my wide curves. I don't have one friend and every man that has tried to show me interest, I've found a way to run him off before he could run off and leave me the same way Daddy left us."

"Oh my God," Her mother sobbed uncontrollably. "Oh my God!"

"Yes, I'm pathetic for resorting to the Internet to meet a man and having to rely on books and my imagination to make me happy. And now that I think I may have met a man who I really like, I realize I hate him, or at least I thought I did. But all you hear is what color his skin is. That's all that matters to you!"

Lenora stood up and walked over to her daughter with her arms outstretched. She wrapped her arms around Laisha and pulled her close to her, the way she remembered her doing many times before her father left. It felt good being in her mother's arms.

"I didn't realize…oh God," Lenora sobbed as she kissed her forehead. "I'm so sorry, baby. I'm so sorry. Father, forgive me!"

Lenora pulled away and stared into her daughter's eyes. "It's time for you to start living, Lai. No matter what I've said to you over the years, you're a beautiful, beautiful girl. Your father's actions were his own, not yours and I am so sorry for taking my pain out on you without even realizing you lost him, too."

"I want us to be friends again Momma. I miss you."

"I love you, baby. But, you need more friends than me. It's time for you to make friends your own age. And if you think this Devin man may be the one, I think you need to at least give the relationship a chance."

"You think so, Momma?"

Lenora cupped her daughter's face in her hands. "I know so."

Lenora and Laisha spent the rest of the weekend bonding and promising to visit each other more often. They even went to mid-day worship service together. When Laisha left on Sunday evening, she called Tinisha and made plans to have lunch with her on Monday. She needed a second opinion about the Devin situation.

<u>Devin</u>

Devin had been emailing Laisha for the past two days. *Maybe I should just leave her alone,* he reasoned. *But, I want her though. I want to love her and show her that I can love her past her pain. Show her that I can love her like a man after God's own heart.* Devin sighed deeply as he opened his account and began typing. *Here I am, sitting here getting ready to send her yet another email.*

TO: <u>Bountifully Blessed Sista@HisLove.com</u>
FROM: <u>Techy4Christ@HisLove.com</u>
SUBJECT: I'd love to talk to you…

Laisha,

Why are you ignoring me? I really don't understand how your feelings can just change. All I do know is that I want you.

With Love,

Devin

Devin closed his eyes for a moment, and then he pressed send. He prayed that he would get a positive response from Laisha. Any response at all.

Devin wasn't a heavy drinker but he found himself popping the top on his third beer of the day.

Chapter Seven
Laisha

Exhausted from her trip home from Asheville, Laisha figured she'd check her email before taking a nap. The first thing she saw was several emails from Devin. Her initial thought was to delete them, but something pressed on her mind, telling her to go ahead and read the messages. She opened the first one and read it before clicking on the second. *Wow, Devin's really persistent,* she thought. After reading the numerous emails, she finally responded to one and told him that she just needed time to think things out and that she would talk to him soon. Satisfied with her response to Devin, Laisha shut down her computer and walked down the hall to her bedroom. She was too exhausted for anything other than sleep.

***

"Hi Tinisha!" Laisha was excited and nervous at the same time. Outside of book club meetings and poetry night afterward, hanging out was new to Laisha.

"Hi Laisha, how are you?" Tinisha hugged Laisha. She was surprised that Laisha called her. Tinisha had given Laisha her number three years ago, hoping that they could hang out and do lunch or something some times, but, Laisha had never called her until now.

"I'm good Tinisha and you?" Laisha was all smiles as the hostess led them to their table.

"I'm hanging girl. I had to run little Nyah to the doctor and Devin to football camp. I was worried that I would be late and not make our lunch date."

"Oh girl, I would have waited for you." Laisha responded as she daydreamed of having little ones of her own to fuss over. "Is Nyah okay, Tinisha?"

"Oh yeah, she's fine it was just time for her twenty-four month old check up."

"Oh okay. As long as she's okay." Laisha was grateful for the waiter heading their way because she really didn't know what else to say. The experience of hanging out was so new to her.

"Hello ladies, may I take your order?" This young chocolate brother flashed his biggest and brightest smile. He was very handsome and it acted as if he knew it. His eyes quickly roamed Laisha's fuller figure before focusing on Tinisha's smaller physique.

Laisha wasn't shocked. She knew that most guys seemed to be attracted to the thinner, prettier women.

"Yes," Tinisha spoke up, "I'll have the grilled chicken salad with extra chicken and honey mustard on the side, and a raspberry iced tea."

Already Laisha was beginning to feel self-conscious. She wanted a juicy steak and a baked potato but figured the waiter expected a woman of her size to eat that and more. Instead of ordering steak, she ordered a salad as well. "I think I'll have the Asian chicken salad and a diet sierra mist."

"Excellent choices ladies," the waiter commented as he retrieved their menus, "I'll be right back with your drinks."

"He's a cutie isn't he?" Laisha thought it was so cool how Tinisha wasn't the least bit shy. She shamelessly watched the little hunk walk away and admired his tight butt.

She held her head down as if she was ashamed to admit that she found someone attractive. What did it matter if he was handsome or not? He wouldn't have given her the time of day. "Yeah, he's handsome."

"Laisha I don't wanna step on your toes or offend you or anything, but why do you hold your head down all the time? You are so beautiful. I wish you would hold your head up."

Laisha was left speechless, finding it impossible to believe that someone as beautiful as Tinisha had such kind words to say to her. She'd never thought herself to be remotely cute, and far from beautiful. For her, compliments came few and far in between.

"Umm…well, I guess it's just something that I've always done. I never really thought about why I do it." She decided not to harp on her mother since they were in the process of mending the fence.

"Well, we're going to work on that," Tinisha stated matter-of-factly.

"Excuse me ladies," the waiter returned with their drinks. "Your salads will be out in just a few minutes. Can I get you anything else?" Both ladies declined and the young man moved over to the next table, flirting with the two young ladies at that table.

"So, who is he?"

"Who's who?" Laisha initially thought Tinisha was referring to the server.

Tinisha smiled coyly, slowly removed her straw from its paper covering, placed it in the glass and took a long sip of tea. "I can see it in your eyes. You've got man trouble. Tell me who he is and what's going on."

"How did you know it was about a man?"

"Well, I know it's not about a book," Tinisha giggled. "Laisha, I know we don't know each other that well, no more than discussing our books of the week and an occasional drink at poetry night, but I sense that you're a good person. I also sense that you hide behind your work to avoid a social life." Laisha nodded affirmatively. "Why?" Tinisha questioned.

"If you looked like me, you'd hide behind work or anything big enough to shield you from the world." Tears welled in her eyes but she refused to cry. Instead she quickly changed the subject. "But, let's not get into that. One reason I called you is because I need advice and yes, it is about a man."

While they waited for their entrees, she gave Tinisha the rundown on her and Devin. It felt like a big weight being lifted off her chest as she shared her feelings about Devin and the dilemma she was facing.

"I don't know what to do," Laisha concluded as the waiter returned and set their plates before them. The food smelled good and looked divine.

"What are you so afraid of?" Tinisha asked while cutting chunks of chicken and taking a big mouthful of her salad.

"If I take a chance on love and Devin ends up leaving me, I'll be devastated, Tinisha. I can't handle that." She slowly drizzled dressing on her salad, picked up her fork and began eating.

"Leave you? Why are you thinking about him leaving you before you even give the relationship a chance?" Laisha shrugged her shoulders and took a quick sip of Sierra Mist.

"Laisha, is your father still in your life?" Tinisha inquired still confused by Laisha's statement. There had to be something deeper going on with Laisha.

She shook her head. "He left us when I was a little girl. I haven't heard from him since."

No wonder she don't trust men, Tinisha reasoned. "Have you ever thought of looking him up? Reaching out to your father may bring you some kind of closure."

"Girl, that door has been closed," she laughed lightly. "Daddy made his choice to leave and that's that. Had he wanted a relationship with me, he could have called me. Instead all he did was send child support checks while Momma struggled to keep a roof over our heads and took her pain and frustrations out on me."

"How's your relationship with your mother now?"

Laisha smiled and answered, "We're working on it. Finally."

"That's great to hear." Tinisha didn't want to push the issue but she wanted her to give serious thought to reuniting with her father. There was no way she'd heal and allow herself to be loved until she resolved things with him. "God is good, maybe you and your father can work things out, too."

She shrugged her shoulders and took another sip of soda. "Maybe."

That was Tinisha's cue to drop the subject. "So, you said the situation with Devin was one reason you invited me here. What's the other reason?"

Laisha laid her fork down on the napkin next to her plate and finished chewing before answering Tinisha. "I've got to come out of hiding some time, right? It's time I make friends."

"Amen!" Tinisha shouted as she and Laisha slapped hi-fives. She then picked up her glass and motioned for Laisha to do the same. "This is to new beginnings."

"To new beginnings," Laisha chimed in as they clinked their glasses together.

Devin

"Devin, may I see you in my office please?"

The sound of Mr. Woodson's booming voice coming across the intercom snapped Devin back to reality. He was supposed to be wrapping up a small assignment, one that shouldn't have taken longer than thirty minutes, yet he'd been procrastinating for hours. His mind was fixed on Laisha and nothing else mattered as much at the time.

"Yes sir, Mr. Woodson." *I hope this is good news,* Devin thought as he stood. He slowly walked down the corridor that led to Mr. Woodson's office. The door to the office was open and Devin knocked as he sauntered into the grand office.

"Good afternoon Mr. Woodson, sir." Mr. Woodson instructed Devin to close the door and take a seat in the chair across from his large oak desk.

"Devin, I have a big assignment for you. Landing the Tyson account can mean millions for our company and I'm entrusting it to you," Mr. Woodson announced.

"Wow, I'm speechless," Devin replied. "Thank you for trusting me to handle such a big account, sir."

"No need to thank me. Your work speaks for itself, Devin." Mr. Woodson picked up a thick manila folder and handed it over to Devin. "I realize Laisha is out sick today, but I want both of you on this account. You're my best employees and together, I know getting this account will be like stealing candy from a baby."

"Mr. Woodson, I'm not sure Laisha will want to…"

"If the two of you pull this off and secure this account for us, there'll be a decent raise and promotion for the both of you." Mr. Woodson rolled his leather chair back, stood up, and extended his hand across his desk. Devin quickly stood up and accepted Mr. Woodson's hand for a firm shake. "Good luck."

Devin dared not attempt another objection. Mr. Woodson's mind was made up. Devin simply thanked him and headed for the door.

"Devin?" He turned to face his employer. "You'll find Ms. Bowman's address in the folder. I'd like you two to start on this assignment right away, today if possible."

"Yes, sir," he eagerly nodded before exiting the office and heading back to his desk. *I can't believe that Mr. Woodson wants us to work together.* Devin hadn't been this excited since the day Abby was born. He couldn't believe he would be able to spend quality time working with his heart's desire. Maybe he could open her up to going on a date, as well.

Devin stopped at his desk long enough to shut everything down and grab his briefcase before taking the elevator to the parking garage where he jumped in his truck and rushed to Laisha's apartment.

<u>**Laisha**</u>

Laisha was in the kitchen preparing to fix herself a bowl of ice cream when the doorbell sounded. "I bet that's Mrs. Akins from next door," she mused as she set the carton of ice cream down on the counter. "She probably wants to borrow a cup of this and a bag of that," she mumbled under her breath while walking to the front door. Expecting to see her elderly neighbor, she flung the front door open and was shocked to see the person on the other side of her threshold was not Mrs. Akins.

"Devin, what are you doing here? How did you get my address? I can't believe you just showed up…"

Devin didn't speak a word. He tossed his briefcase to the floor and grabbed her in a warm and tight embrace. Telling Laisha how badly he wanted her had gotten him nowhere so Devin decided to show her. She tried to pull away from him but the feel of his arms wrapped around her, was too much for her to resist. She melted into him, laid her head on his shoulder and cried.

"Devin, can I ask you something?" she inquired.

"Anything," he replied as he snuggled his closer to her.

"How did you get my address?"

Devin laughed and held her back, at arms' length upright. He'd almost forgotten about the assignment. Finally seeing Laisha made everything else seem unimportant.

"Mr. Woodson has assigned us to the Tyson account. He wants us to work together on it and get started right away."

Had she heard him correctly? "The John Tyson account? Are you kidding me? That's the biggest account in this area, I've been praying a long time for an account like that."

"I know. Mr. Woodson said it could bring in millions and we'd be up for a raise and promotion if we get the job done."

"Wow! I can't believe it!" She flung her arms around Devin's neck. "Let's get to work."

"Now?" Devin asked. He was hoping to spend the time getting to know the woman he felt God had sent him, and him alone.

She was already slipping her hair back into a ponytail, and putting on her glasses, getting ready to get to work. "Yes, I'm ready to get started. This could be big for both our careers."

"No, it wasn't," he quickly assured her. "Not at all." Reluctantly, he retrieved his briefcase and sat next to her on the sofa. "Let's get to work."

"Devin, there'll be plenty of time for dating." She kissed his cheek. "I promise."

Devin pulled her closer to him. "I knew you wanted me all along," he teased.

Chapter Eight
Devin

In the weeks that followed, Devin watched Laisha transform into a totally different woman. She was no longer the angry co-worker who sat across from him at the office wearing those dull basic colors; she now wore her bright yellows, oranges, and pinks. In fact, they spent most of their time together working outside the office, wining and dining their potential client. The two were together constantly. Only separating to go home and sleep, and occasionally when Tinisha and Laisha got together for lunch, shopping, and their weekly book club meeting.

Laisha had met and fallen in love with Abby and Devin couldn't have been more pleased to have his two leading ladies getting along so well. Life was perfect in his world. His relationship with God, love, family, and career were all in sync and the best was yet to come.

Esteban usually picked Abby up on Sundays but this particular day Morgan came by. The pregnancy had only enhanced her beauty and the expectant mother was glowing. She looked radiant in an oversized tee-shirt and maternity jeans. Her golden curls flowed down her back and past her shoulders.

Devin was helping Abby pack when the doorbell rang.

"Laisha, will you get the door, please? It's probably Abby's stepfather!"

"Sure, no problem," Laisha said as she saved her document and waltzed over to the door. She'd met Esteban before and found him to be a pleasant man. She really liked him.

"Hello," Laisha said when she opened the door and found a beautiful, blonde bombshell standing there cheesing like Miss America. The woman looked like a runway model despite the little bump in her belly.

"Hi, I'm Morgan." The woman extended her hand toward Laisha. "I'm Abby's mother. You must be Laisha."

"Yes, I am," she replied as the two shook hands. "It's nice to meet you."

"It's nice to finally meet you. Abby talks about you all the time."

"Mommy!" Abby squealed as she ran into the living room and past Laisha. Her mother squatted and the two embraced. "I've missed you!"

"I missed you, too, Sweet Pea!"

"Miss Laisha, this is my mommy. She's going to have a baby real soon. That means I'm going to be a big sister," Abby proudly announced.

"Is that right? Congratulations." Laisha felt awkward in Morgan's presence. How could Devin want her after being with someone so beautiful? She and the woman were like night and day; no pun intended about race, but seriously, they couldn't have been more different physically.

Morgan was tall and slender, and even pregnant her waist wasn't as thick as her's. It was obvious by her mannerism that Morgan was confident, not cocky, but confident in her beauty.

"Thank you," Morgan replied. She then looked past Laisha and spoke to Devin who was walking toward the trio. "How are you Devin?"

"I'm doing well, Morgan. How are you?" He greeted her with a quick peck on the cheek. It was a friendly kiss but Laisha immediately felt threatened. She was thankful when her cell phone rang.

"Excuse me," she whispered. She retrieved her phone, answered it, and disappeared into the bedroom.

"I'm good, had a great time with Miss Abby this weekend," he answered, playfully squeezing Abby's nose. "How is Esteban?"

"He's good, out of town on business today." Her statement was followed by an awkward silence. "Well, we better get going. Tell Laisha it was very nice meeting her. She's very beautiful, Devin."

"Thank you Morgan. I'll be sure to tell her." He kissed his daughter good-bye and watched them disappear into the elevator before closing the door.

"Devin, guess what?" Laisha squealed.

"What?"

"We landed the Tyson account! That was Mr. Woodson calling with the good news. He wants us in his office first thing tomorrow morning!"

"Are you serious?" Devin was so excited he rushed over and picked Laisha up, spinning her around in his arms.

"Yes, I'm serious!"

"Let's go celebrate, right now. Dinner is on me. You wanna invite Tinisha and her husband to celebrate with us?" Devin had placed her feet back onto the floor and was already grabbing for his jacket.

"You know, Devin, I'm kind of tired. We've been working hard these past few weeks." She began gathering her notes and stuffed everything into her briefcase. "I think I'm going to head home and get a good night's rest."

"Laisha, what's wrong?" Devin immediately sensed she was upset about something.

"Nothing," she lied, feigning a weak smile.

"Laisha, come on now. We've come a long way in these past few weeks. Don't shut down on me now."

"Devin, what do you want with me? It's obvious you can have any woman you want. Why me?"

"What do you mean, what do I want with you? Laisha, I care a lot about you. In fact, I think I've fallen in love with you. You're beautiful, smart, feisty, and most importantly, you love the Lord."

She laughed as tears welled in her eyes. "After being with someone as beautiful as Morgan, how can you even think you're in love with me? Look at me, Devin. How long will it take before you leave me for someone who looks like your ex?"

"Is that what this is about? You're still insecure so you're looking for a way out. Well, I'm not letting you go that easy, Laisha." Devin tried to snatch the briefcase out of her hand but she stepped back. "Laisha, please, don't do this."

"Devin, it's already done. We had a good time together, but I know you can't really love someone like me. Let's just end things amicably so we can continue to work together with no animosity. Okay?"

"You gave me the best of you and now you want to just snatch it away? What is wrong with you, Laisha?"

Walking away with her head down, she opened his front door and said, "See you at the office tomorrow, Devin. Good night."

Laisha

"You did what?"

Tinisha screamed so loudly into the phone that Laisha had to remove the phone from her ear.

"I broke it off with him before he could break it off with me," she repeated. "If you'd seen his ex you'd know why, Tinisha. The woman is gorgeous. Now what would Devin want with me after being married to someone so beautiful. Trust, it's only a matter of time before he finds him another dime piece to show off, especially now that we've been promoted."

Laisha was eating a big bowl of her homemade banana pudding while sitting in front of the TV watching *House*. The USA network was airing her favorite episode, the one with Mos Def when he was trapped inside his own body, not able to communicate with anyone. That's how she felt, trapped.

"Did he say this or did you just ASSUME it for him?"

"I'm right on this, Tinisha. I know I am."

"Lord have mercy. Laisha, I saw a light in you. Dating Devin brought out something magical in you. If I saw it, I know you felt it. Are you really telling me you're going to give that up because you think his ex-wife is more beautiful than you?"

"I know she's more beautiful, Tinisha. Morgan is more beautiful than Cindy Crawford. I can't compete with that."

"Duh, it's not a competition, Laisha! Devin and Morgan are divorced, she's remarried, and he chose you! He's not trying to get back with Morgan. The man has been breaking his neck to get you and you're throwing it all away. Why can't you see the beauty in yourself that everyone else sees?"

"But, Tinisha you don't understand-"

"Oh, yes, I do! You need to call your mother and try to track your father down. Until you meet with him and close that door, you're going to continue to sabotage every relationship you enter into. So, call your mother and call me back *after* you talk to your father."

Tinisha bid Laisha a good night before hanging up the phone. She was angry and didn't want to say anything that would hurt her friend's feelings. Tinisha meant to be firm but knowing how sensitive she was, she didn't want to go overboard and push her back into that tiny shell of a life she had once embraced.

Laisha wasn't convinced that her father really had anything to do with it but she decided what the hell and took a deep breath before picking up the phone to dial her mother's number.

"Hello?" Lenora answered after a few short rings.

"Momma, hey!"

"Lai, how you doing baby? I hope you're calling about visiting soon. I'm ready to meet Devin. He's always so nice on the phone. Maybe y'all can come visit the weekend and come to church with me on Sunday. I can't wait to show off your new fellow."

"Maybe," she said, not wanting to tell her mother about their abrupt breakup. Lenora had finally warmed up to the idea of her daughter dating a non-Black. As a matter of fact, Lenora was quite fond of Devin and always had kind words for him. "But, what I called for was to see if you had a number for daddy."

"For who?" She knew her mother heard her. Her father just wasn't a subject they discussed, not until now. They couldn't keep putting it off, she had finally realized that.

"Daddy. I need to try and find my father, Momma."

"Why? You haven't needed him in all these years. Why now?" Lenora wasn't ready to share her baby with anyone, not even Jimmy.

"Momma, I don't have time to explain it right now, but if you have his number, or anyone's number who can help me find him, I really need that information. Please, Momma."

"Oh, okay. Hold on, Laisha." Her mother laid the phone down and two minutes felt like two hours to her as she sat staring at the wall. *For all I know my father is dead. What am I supposed to do if he's dead?*

"You still there?" Her mother asked.

"Yes, Momma. Did you find the number?" She was on pins and needles, growing more and more nervous with each passing second.

"I don't know how good the number is but yes, I found it. It's 555-9876."

"What's the area code?"

"404."

"404? You mean my father lives in the Atlanta area?" Laisha couldn't believe it. Her father lived so close and she'd never once run into him. He was so close and he'd never tried to find her.

"According to your Aunt Janet, yes, he does. But you be careful, Laisha. He walked out on you once and never looked back. I've had this number for awhile now but I was afraid to share it with you. I didn't want to get your hopes up only to have him let you down again. Don't let him hurt you again, baby."

"I won't Momma. I just need-well, I just need to see him and get some closure. Thanks, Momma."

"I love you. You call me soon, okay?"

"I love you, too and yes ma'am, I'll call you in a couple days."

She hung up the phone and stared at the phone number she'd written down for five minutes before she mustered up the courage to dial it. *What am I supposed to say to this man?*

"Hello?" The sound of her father's deep voice brought tears to her eyes.

"Daddy?"

Chapter Nine
Devin

"Job well done, Devin!" Mr. Woodson congratulated him. "You and Ms. Bowman are not only getting a raise and promotion, you're getting a hefty bonus."

"Thank you, Mr. Woodson." Moving into his new office was bittersweet for Devin. The view of downtown Atlanta was exquisite but his mind was elsewhere. He'd looked forward to seeing Laisha this morning but was told she'd called in sick. He knew she was avoiding him and Devin had a good mind to drive over to her apartment. Unfortunately, his promotion meant more new clients to tackle and Mr. Woodson had already assigned him to another major account to win over to their team.

"No, thank you. Maybe you should take Ms. Bowman a fruit basket after work, break the good news to her about the bonus. That should make her feel better."

"I think I will."

Devin put his best foot forward all day, trying his best not to think about Laisha. She wasn't answering her phone or emails he sent to her during lunch. At the end of the day, Devin decided to run to Wal-Mart and purchase a fruit basket as suggested by Mr. Woodson.

When he arrived at Laisha's apartment, he rang the doorbell and knocked for twenty solid minutes before giving up. He knew she was inside. Her elderly neighbor came out onto her porch as Devin was walking back to his vehicle.

"You must be Laisha's new fellow?" she inquired.

"Yes, ma'am."

"She must be mad at you then. She's at home, left for lunch and was back about an hour later, hasn't left since." Devin smiled and nodded. The older woman had no shame about her nosiness. "Whatever you done must've been mighty bad if she won't open the door for a handsome fellow such as yourself."

"Thank you ma'am." He was about to climb into his truck with the fruit basket but decided against it. He wasn't going to do anything with it so he decided to leave it with the nosy neighbor. "Miss, would you care for a fruit basket?"

"Oh, why thank you young man!" Devin walked up the steps and handed Mrs. Akins the basket. "I'm rooting for you. That girl works too much. When she ain't working, her nose is buried in a book, shut up inside that house. She hardly ever comes out and gets any fresh air. I'm going to pray for you two because I think you're a good fellow for her."

"Thank you Ms.-"

"Akins. Wilma Akins."

"Thank you Mrs. Akins. I need all the prayer I can get with this one."

Mrs. Akins walked closer to him and motioned for him to lean in closer. She looked over her shoulder and whispered, "Pray for me, too." She paused long enough to laugh and nod toward the window where Mr. Atkins was standing and waving. "He has Alzheimer's and its hard keeping up with him some times. And not to mention, some idiot doctor prescribed him Viagra! That man chases me all around the house when he remembers he has those little happy pills."

That was more information than Devin had wanted to hear. "You're definitely in my prayers, Mrs. Akins. Definitely."

Devin waved good-bye to the couple before leaving.

Chapter Ten
Laisha

What was I thinking when I agreed to have dinner with this man?

Her heart raced as she sat in the booth watching the burning candle that set atop the wooden table. Other patrons talked, laughed, and interacted as they ate their meals. Her hands shaking, she turned her wrist up and glanced at her watch for the umpteenth time. *If he's not here in five minutes, I'm out of here.* She picked up her half-empty champagne flute and brought the glass to her rose colored lips. Closing her eyes, she took a sip of her favorite white wine and savored the dry sweetness.

"Laisha, you look beautiful." Her eyes quickly fluttered open at the sound of his voice and as she stared up at him, tears welled in her eyes.

"Daddy?" he looked the same with the exception of the salt and pepper hair, mustache, and goatee. Father time had been kind to Jimmy Bowman and in her eyes he was still the most handsome man in the world. Tears cascaded down her cheeks as she took in his almond shaped eyes, wide nose, and full lips. His dark skin hadn't one wrinkle, still smooth as whipped chocolate.

"In the flesh," he laughed, stretching his arms wide for an embrace, she slid out of the booth and into her father's arms where she melted into his chest. His cologne tickled her nostrils and she smiled at the remembrance of his scent, Old Spice. She'd always loved that smell on her father and anytime her sense of smell came in contact with Old Spice, Laisha found herself searching high and low, hoping to catch a small glimpse of him.

Her body began to shake uncontrollably as she sobbed into her father's chest, allowing herself to feel an array of emotions; she was happy to see him, angry that he'd been out of her life for so long, and scared that he might not accept her and would leave her again. She couldn't handle that because what she needed most right now was to be able to trust men again, trust herself to love and be loved without worrying and anticipating heartache and pain. She couldn't fathom a relationship with Devin or any one for that matter until her issues with her father were resolved.

"I have so many questions, Daddy, I don't even know where to begin," she whispered.

Jimmy pulled away from his daughter and stared into her tear-filled eyes and she saw that he, too, was crying. A small smile formed in the corner of her lips as she realized that her father did love her and had missed her.

"We can start by sitting down and ordering dinner," he suggested, she slid back into the booth and her father sat opposite her. "And Baby, there's nothing you can't ask me. I'll answer your questions honestly."

After the server took their orders, Laisha took a long sip from the wine flute before placing the glass back down on the small coaster. She stared at her father and decided to start the interrogation.

"Why did you leave us?"

Resting his elbows on the table, Jimmy leaned forward. He placed his hands down, palms up on the table and motioned for her to place her hands in his. She did so and he squeezed them affectionately just as he'd done every night they prayed together so many years earlier.

"I won't make any excuses, Laisha, and I won't blame your mother because it's not her fault. I made the decision to have extramarital affairs throughout our marriage and I allowed that weakness to ruin my marriage. Don't get me wrong I did love Connie, because regardless of skin color, she, like your mother, was a good woman. I just was not the type of man to do right by a woman, even when I tried, I fell short."

He took a deep sigh and closed his eyes, hoping to choke back the tears that welled in his eyes. When he opened his eyes again, he saw his beautiful daughter staring at him and he couldn't help smiling at her. She was a spitting image of him, the dark skin, almond shaped eyes, and full lips. As a woman, she possessed that softness that made her beautiful like his mother and sisters, and with her hair in a French roll with a few curls dangling about her round face, she just was stunning.

"Baby, I thought I was doing you and your mother a favor by leaving. I didn't want to keep hurting her and as you grew older, I didn't want you thinking that was how relationships were supposed to be. I didn't deserve you and your mother."

"But, I deserved to have my daddy in my life. You have no idea how many times I thought about you and wondered if you were alive or dead. I didn't understand what I did to drive you away. And momma," Laisha bit her bottom lip and shook her head as more tears spilled over. "She was so angry when you left. I thought she hated me because every day of my life, I had to hear how much I looked like you and how fat I was. It was so hard and I knew things would have been different if you hadn't left."

"Lenora was a strong woman and I guess I figured she could endure me leaving and even appreciate it after all I'd put her through. I had no idea she'd turn her resentment for me toward you. I hope you don't hate her for it though, I'd rather you hate me because I caused that pain and anger."

"Daddy, I don't hate either one of you," she whispered through trembling lips. "I just hate how screwed up my heart is because of all that happened." Laisha went on to tell her father about Devin and how she wanted to give their love a try but was afraid to because she feared at some point he, too, would leave her.

"I don't know this Devin guy but I know one thing for sure, you can't hide from love and there are no guarantees that you won't get hurt, Laisha. That's just the chance we take when we fall in love. Even if you get hurt, you have to pick yourself up and when you go into another relationship, you're wiser from experience." Jimmy smiled and squeezed his daughter's hands once again. "I want you to follow your heart and if it has lead you to Devin, don't allow fear to turn you away from what could be the greatest love of your life."

"Aww Daddy," Laisha cried as she slid out the booth and flung her arms around her first love. "Thank you. Thank you so much."

"You don't owe me any thanks. I'm the one who is thankful because you could have easily allowed me to remain dead in your life. I know I can't make up for the years I've missed being your father, but I'm here now, Lai, and until God takes me away, I ain't going no place." He kissed her forehead tenderly. "If that

Devin is fool enough to hurt my baby girl, his tail is grass and Daddy is the lawn mower."

Devin

The ringing of the phone awakened Devin from his nap on the couch. He jumped to his feet and ran toward his computer desk where the phone lay.

"Hello?" he answered.

"Hey, it's me."

His heart fluttered and his knees buckled at the sound of her angelic voice. Devin took a seat at his computer and exhaled.

"Laisha, it's so good to hear your voice. I have been thinking about you every waking minute and dreaming of you every time I close my eyes."

"I've been thinking about you as well, Devin." Laisha cleared her throat. "I miss you and I'm so sorry for everything. I know I've been pushing you away but I really care about you, Devin. I think I love you."

He felt swelling in his heart when she proclaimed her love for him. "Baby, I know I love you. If there are two people in this world I love, it's you and Abby. I don't ever want to lose either of you, Laisha; not ever again."

"I can't promise I'll be perfect Devin. I still have issues and…"

"Laisha, nobody is perfect and no relationship is perfect. All I can promise is my love and respect, and loyalty to you. And that's all I dare ask of you in return. Can we at least have that Baby?"

"Yes. I think that's a start," she agreed.

"You have no idea how much I've been missing you, girl," Devin laughed into the phone. "You were wrong for loving me and leaving me."

Laisha laughed, "As badly as I have missed you, I'm on my way."

"Drive safely, baby," Devin said before hanging up the phone.

With twenty minutes to spare, he jumped up from the chair and straightened up the apartment. Devin put in his favorite Luther Vandross CD and lit vanilla candles throughout the house.

Laisha

Standing outside Devin's door, she heard soft music playing and smelled vanilla creeping from under the door's frame. Her heart warmed as she rang the doorbell and she ached for Devin's embraced.

"Oh baby, wow," Devin said when he flung the door open and saw Laisha standing there in a pair of stilettos and a wrap dress.

Laisha stepped across the threshold and giggled. She'd never dreamed of having a man feel this way, but had to admit that she felt beautiful as Devin's eyes combed her curves.

When Devin didn't move she cleared her throat and asked, "Aren't you going to be a gentleman and invite me in?"

Devin shook his head, snapping out of his daze. She had him mesmerized from the minute he opened the door and saw her standing there in those black, three-inch stilettos and that black dress that left everything to his imagination.

"Of course I am. Where are my manners?" He walked behind her and rested his hands on her shoulders, gently massaging them. He rested his face against her neck and allowed her sweet smell to intoxicate his senses. "You smell good, baby. Laisha, I love you."

"I love you so much, Devin," she proudly proclaimed.

"I don't know what's gotten into you but I like it," Devin commented.

She turned on her side and propped up on her elbow, "You got in here. In my heart," she confessed. "At first, I was scared because of the race thing. I knew my mother hated interracial relationships since my father left her for his white lover and I didn't want to face that. I also thought I hated you because we were always down each other's throats at work." She playfully wrapped her hands around his throat and pretended to choke him.

"But, the real, true reason I was so afraid is because my father left me and I thought you'd leave me, too, Devin." She allowed her head to fall into his chest and she listened intently to the beating of his heart. "I've been running from love all my life."

"So, what changed your mind and made you stop running?" Devin nestled his chin into the top of her head and caressed her back.

"You, Tinisha, and my father. You were so persistent about giving us a chance and Tinisha made me realize that I should contact my father and face the past. It was the only way I'd be able to move on. I was hesitant at first and just tried to make us work, but as you can see, that wasn't the answer." She paused long enough to place a tender kiss on his lips and then continued. "After I ran away from you, I finally tracked my father down and had dinner with him."

"Baby, that's wonderful. How did it go?"

She shrugged her shoulders and cuddled closer to him. "I'm here so I guess it went pretty well."

"Well, I'm proud of you." Devin pushed forward until they were both sitting in a upright position. He kissed her on her full lips and hopped to his feet.

"Where are you going? What's wrong?" she questioned when he put on his shoes and grabbed for his keys.

"Nothing's wrong. I just thought I'd grab us a quick bite to eat." Devin winked his right eye at his baby. He then kneeled in front of her. "And if you think for one minute I'm walking out that door and not coming back to you, you're crazy." They kissed and he asked, "Now, what do you want to eat?"

"I could go for a juicy cheeseburger with fries and a Dr. Pepper." She rubbed her rumbling stomach and laughed. "I'm really hungry."

"Any dessert for you?" he asked.

"No thank you my love."

"Promise me something, Laisha."

"What's that?"

"That you'll be my wife in the near future. I know it's early on to officially propose but I love you and I know without a doubt that God has destined me to spend the rest of my life with you."

She didn't even have to think about her answer to him. Laisha replied, "I can't wait to be Mrs. Devin Kingston.

Devin kissed her, jumped to his feet, and did a celebratory dance that made Laisha laugh until her stomach ached. She loved that corny side of him; she loved all of him.

"Okay, I'm going to get the food and we can make plans for this weekend when I come back. It's my weekend to have Abby and I want the three of us to have a blast."

"I look forward to it. Abby is such an amazing child."

"And together, we're going to make about two or three more amazing kids so their big sister can help us spoil them rotten."

Her eyes twinkled like stars on a moonless night at the mention of kids. "I'm going to hold you to that, Baby." She was ready, finally ready for love and all that it entailed.

"Be back in a few." She watched Devin as he walked out the door, confident that he'd return. Laisha didn't worry about what may be in their future; she focused on making the best of the present and vowed to God that she would never run from love again.

HisLove.com, Laisha thought as she smiled to herself and went about the task of blowing out candles and straightening up *her* man's apartment.

Chapter Ten
Six Months Later

"I never thought this day would come. Me walking my beautiful daughter down the aisle."

"Daddy, you're going to make me cry and after spending three hours on this make-up, I can't afford to cry.

"I know that's right," Lenora and Tinisha chimed in unison.

"And Lenora, you look as beautiful as you did when we met thirty-five years ago."

Lenora waved her hand dismissively but couldn't help blushing. She was still very much in love with her ex and the two had gone on a few dates. Laisha was praying that her parents would find their way back together in God's time.

Laisha was in awe of the fact that she was about to marry the love of her life. "Momma…I'm really getting married?"

"You are getting married, sweetness", and with that Lenora began to cry.

"Oh Momma, don't cry…" She hugged her mother.

"I'm happy girl, don't be telling me what to do!" Her mother smiled through her tears.

"Oh Momma, this is the best day of my life!"

"I remember the best day of my life, sweetheart." Lenora looked at her daughter, reminiscing on the day that her precious baby girl was born.

"It was the best day of both of our lives." Jimmy chimed in. "We both love you so much."

Just then the music began to play and Tinisha and Abby took their places and began to proceed Laisha and her parents down the aisle. She felt extremely special having both of her parents escort her down the aisle together, to her that meant almost as much as the man who was waiting on her at the front of the church. She felt her heart swell with joy and she began thanking God that she was wearing waterproof mascara, because soft tears of joy began to flow.

Etta James' "At Last," began to play as Laisha and her parents stood in the entryway to the sanctuary. She looked up and saw Devin's smiling face beckoning to her, and that was all she needed to make her way up the aisle. She was so excited that she almost left her parents behind as they made their way through the wedding march. Her heart was beating so fast. *Devin looks so handsome,* she thought. *It still feels like a dream, I can't believe all of this is for me!*

A gorgeous assortment of different color pink roses with ivory baby's breaths was everywhere you looked. It was a beautiful setting and she felt her most beautiful in a pale ivory gown embroidered in baby pink miniature roses on the bottom of her gown and lining her ten foot train. This was definitely a dream come true for Laisha. She was marrying her dream man, in her dream wedding ceremony.

As she finally made it to the front of the church, Devin took her hand, stroking it and whispered, "You look so beautiful." He looked her in her eyes and she wanted to melt. She prayed that she always felt this way whenever her husband looked her in her eyes. If this was just a dream, she most definitely did not want to wake up. She squeezed his hand back and she just knew that this is what heaven must feel like. Love so pure, love so real. Then the pastor began to speak.

"Beloved family and friends, we are here today to witness the blessed union of Laisha Marie Bowman and Devin Ryan Kingston. What God has joined together, let no man, let no woman put asunder. Let us pray." After the pastor went into the most heartfelt prayer that the two had ever heard, he finally asked the age old question, "Who gives this woman away?"

His chest puffed up with the most pride he ever felt in his life, Jimmy proudly answered, "her beautiful mother and I do." He kissed Laisha on her cheek, and shook Devin's hand, and escorted Lenora, who was silently sobbing at this point, to their seat. She passed her flowers to Tinisha as Devin took both of her hands in his and they turned to face each other, as the pastor continued. "The couple have written their own vows and would like to share them with each other and God at this time."

Tears were beginning to line the brim of Devin's eyes as he began to read the most important words his heart ever had to say, "Laisha my love, you are my heart, you are my soul. You have brought so much joy to not just my life, but, to Abby's life as well. Sweetheart, I love the way you love. When you agreed to be my wife, I knew that there really was a God and that he loved me so much, that he created you, just for me. I promise to always be faithful to you and to God. I love you with everything that I am Laisha, and I thank God for you. Thank you for loving me." He kissed her tear-streaked cheek and wiped at her tears as she began to read her vows from her heart to his.

"Devin, you are such a blessing. I know that you were sent to me from up above. I thank God for sending me an angel named Devin to love. I love you with my heart; I need you with soul. As long as I have you and God by my side I know I'm whole. I love you with everything that I am and even everything that I am not. I love the way you love me, Devin. I now know what love is, in its purest and most rare form. I was blind, but your love helped me to see. I promise to love and cherish you and Abby, all of my days."

"With all that has been said here, there really isn't anything else to say. By the powers vested in me, by God and the state of Georgia, I now pronounce you husband and wife. Devin you may kiss your beautiful bride."

Devin threw her veil back, cupped his wife's beautiful face, and kissed her with everything he had within his soul. Laisha swore she felt their souls become one at that very moment and who would have thought it all started with **HisLove.com**.

Acknowledgments

First and foremost, I give all glory and honor to God who is the head of my life. Thank you Father for sending your son Jesus Christ to die on the cross for our sins.

I want to thank my husband who has supported me as I've given up writing erotic romance and committed to writing love stories for the Lord. Jay, I love you now and forever.

Thank you to my parents for all of your love and support.

Thanks to my sister of the pen, Linda R. Herman, for being you. For writing stories that capture the heart, impact the mind and touch our souls. I love you Sis!

A very special thank you to my editor, who always makes sure I dot my I's and cross my T's.

To anyone I may have forgotten to mention, charge it to my head and not my heart. I do thank you.

Love,
    Allyson

Allyson is an author, editor and graphic designer who loves what she does. She has a degree in Medical Office Administration, with a minor degree in Business English.

Ms. Deese resides in Asheville, NC with her husband and family. Visit her online at www.allysonmdeese.com.

Made in the USA
Lexington, KY
12 October 2012